I Don't Believe It, Archie!

ANDREW NORRISS

ILLUSTRATED BY Hannah Shaw

I DON'T BELIEVE IT, ARCHIE!
DAVID FICKLING BOOKS 978 1 849 92080 3

First published in Great Britain by David Fickling Books,
a division of Random House Children's Publishers UK
A Random House Group Company

Hardback edition published 2011
Paperback edition published 2012

1 3 5 7 9 10 8 6 4 2

The Random House Group Limited supports the Forest Stewardship
Council (FSC®), the leading international forest certification organization.
Our books carrying the FSC label are printed on FSC®-certified paper.
FSC is the only forest certification scheme endorsed by the leading
environmental organizations, including Greenpeace. Our paper procurement
policy can be found at www.randomhouse.co.uk/environment.

MIX
Paper from
responsible sources
FSC® C016897

Set in 13/18pt Baskerville

DAVID FICKLING BOOKS
31 Beaumont Street, Oxford, OX1 2NP

www.kidsatrandomhouse.co.uk
www.totallyrandombooks.co.uk
www.randomhouse.co.uk

Addresses for companies within The Random House Group Limited can be found at:
www.randomhouse.co.uk/offices.htm

THE RANDOM HOUSE GROUP Limited Reg. No. 954009

A CIP catalogue record for this book is available from the British Library.

Printed and bound by CPI Group (UK) Ltd, Croydon, CR0 4YY

Also by Andrew Norriss:

Archie's Unbelievably Freaky Week

Aquila
Aquila 2

Ctrl-Z
The Portal
The Unluckiest Boy in the World
The Touchstone
Bernard's Watch
Matt's Million

Woof! A Twist in the Tale
Woof! The Tale Gets Longer
Woof! The Tale Wags On

I dedicate this book to all those children who live quiet, uneventful lives where nothing much out of the ordinary ever seems to happen. If you don't know already, let me tell you how lucky you are . . .

1. On Monday . . .

On Monday, when Archie had been sent out to post a letter, something rather odd happened.

He was halfway down the hill that led to the post office when he heard a rumbling noise, turned round, and saw a piano coming down the middle of the road. There was nobody with it. It was just a large, upright piano, trundling down the hill all on its own.

Archie was surprised, though probably not as surprised as you or I would be, because odd things happened to Archie every day. Some very odd things. As you will see.

While he watched, the piano slowed down, veered slightly over to one side of the road, and then stopped.

When he went over for a closer look, he heard a voice.

'I don't believe it!' said the voice. 'What am I supposed to do now?'

Looking round the end of the piano, Archie saw a girl about his own age, sitting in the front passenger seat of a small car.

'I'm stuck, aren't I!' said the girl. 'How am

I supposed to get out?'

The car she was sitting in only had two doors and it had been parked so that one of them was right up

against a lamp post. The other one was now blocked by the piano.

'Could you move it or something?' asked the girl.

'I don't think so,' said Archie. He was not very big and it was quite a heavy piano.

'Well, could you go and tell my mum what's happened?' asked the girl. She pointed to a house on the other side of the road. 'She's in there. Number sixteen.'

Archie thought about it. 'You want me to go in there . . .'

'Just tell anyone you see that Cyd is trapped in a car,' said the girl. 'They all know me.'

'Right,' said Archie. 'OK . . .'

He crossed the road, walked up a path, and found the front door of number sixteen was open. In the hallway inside, a woman was talking on the phone.

'But he promised to have that piano delivered by ten o'clock!' she was saying. 'How

am I supposed to give singing lessons without a piano . . . ? Well, could you find out, please . . . ? Thank you!'

She put down the phone and saw Archie in the doorway. 'What do you want?' she asked impatiently.

'I'm sorry to bother you,' said Archie, 'but Cyd asked me to tell you—'

'Sid?' the woman frowned. 'You have a message from Sid? Is it about my piano?'

'Well,' Archie hesitated, 'I suppose it could be.' He pointed outside. 'You see, the piano out there is blocking the—'

'What is my piano doing in the middle of the road?' interrupted the woman, staring out through the doorway.

'Well . . .' said Archie.

'Oh, never mind!' The woman had turned on her heel. 'I'll find someone to bring it inside.' And she strode off down the hallway and was gone.

Archie went back to the girl in the car. He thought she might like to know that someone was coming to move the piano, but he found when he got there that the girl had already got someone else to help.

'I'm just going to push the car forward a bit,' said an elderly man in a green raincoat, 'so that your friend can get out. It won't take a moment!'

Archie stood out of the way on the pavement, while the man pushed the car. It rolled forward very easily and was soon at a point where Cyd could have opened either of the doors.

'All right!' said the man. 'You can put the brake on now.'

'Put it on what?' asked the girl.

The car, Archie noticed, was still rolling forward.

'The brake!' said the man. 'The handle beside your seat. You need to pull it!'

Archie could see the girl in the car reach for the brake handle and pull on it, but the car did not stop. It had got to a steep bit of the hill and was, if anything, going faster.

'You have to pull it harder than that!' shouted the man, running alongside the car. 'Come on! Pull!'

'I'm pulling it as hard as I can!' the girl shouted back. 'It's not working!'

She sounded frightened and Archie could see why. The car was still picking up speed and, directly in front of it, further down the road, was an enormous lorry. If the car crashed into it . . .

The man in the green raincoat could see what might happen as well and, at the last minute,

he
pulled open
the car door, leaped
inside while the car was still moving

and a second later it screeched to a halt just inches from the back of the lorry.

Archie, watching, gave a sigh of relief. Or rather, half a sigh, because he could see that, although the car was no longer going to crash, something even worse was about to happen. The back of the lorry was tipping up and, before Archie could so much as shout a warning, there was a great roar and several tons of small stones poured out and engulfed the car. One moment there was a car with two people in it, the next it had disappeared under an enormous heap of gravel.

Archie was already running down the pavement. He got there just in time to see the lorry driving away, while the car was completely buried.

'Are you all right?' he called, and was relieved to hear a faint reply.

'Help!' said a tiny voice. 'Get help!'

'All right!' said Archie. 'Don't worry. I'll get someone!'

He looked round.
There were some
men on the
building
site

behind him who would probably be able to
help, but even better, he noticed, there was a
policeman walking down the road from the
top of the hill. He would know what to do.

Archie ran back up the road, to where
the policeman was talking to a man in brown
overalls.

'You've lost a piano?' the policeman was
saying.

'I was delivering it to number sixteen,' said
the man, 'at the top of the hill. But the woman

9

there said she hadn't ordered any piano and—'

'Excuse me,' said Archie, breathlessly.

'Hang on a minute, lad,' said the policeman. 'One thing at a time.' He turned back to the man in the brown overalls. 'You were saying?'

'Well, I went inside to phone the boss,' said the man, 'and when I came out the piano had gone! Just . . . vanished!'

'Where's my husband!' An elderly woman in a knitted hat had come out of her house and was looking anxiously up and down the pavement. 'What's happened to my husband?'

'Please!' said the policeman. 'I'm attending to this gentleman at the moment.'

'But you don't understand!' said the woman in the knitted hat. 'My husband said he'd wait for me here, and he's disappeared!

Where's he gone!'

'I think,' said Archie, 'that I might be able to—'

'I told you to wait your turn,' said the policeman, sharply. 'I can only deal with one thing at a time and—'

'*Aaaaaagh!*' A woman in jeans and a T-shirt was running across the road. 'Cyd!' she screamed. 'What's happened to Cyd!'

'Who?' The policeman was beginning to look rather flustered.

'My daughter! I left her out here in the car, and she's gone!' The woman looked wildly up and down the road. 'She was sitting in the car right here and now she's gone. Somebody's stolen my daughter!'

'It's like the Bermuda Triangle,

isn't it?' said the man in the brown overalls. 'All these people and things disappearing!' He looked at Archie. 'I lost a piano!'

'I know,' said Archie. 'And if someone would just listen to me—'

'I'm telling you for the last time,' said the policeman, 'just keep quiet until I'm ready, will you?' He turned to the woman in jeans. 'You say your daughter's gone missing?'

'And the car!' said the woman. 'The car's gone too! Somebody's driven off with her!'

Archie's father had always told him that it was rude to interrupt when other people were talking, but he thought, on this occasion, he had no choice.

'YOU HAVE TO LISTEN TO ME!' he shouted. 'BECAUSE I KNOW WHERE EVERYONE IS! I KNOW WHAT'S HAPPENED!'

There was a brief moment of silence.

'You know where the girl is?' said the policeman.

12

'And my husband?' said the woman in the knitted hat.

'And my piano?' said the man in the brown overalls.

'Yes, I do,' said Archie. He turned to the woman in jeans and a T-shirt. 'Your daughter, Cyd, is under those stones.' He pointed down the hill to the pile of gravel.

The woman went very pale and swayed slightly as if she was going to faint.

'And if your husband was wearing a green raincoat . . .' – Archie had turned to the elderly woman in the knitted hat – '. . . you'll find he's under there as well.'

The elderly woman's hands flew to her mouth and she gave a little cry.

'You're saying there's two people buried under that pile of gravel?' asked the policeman.

'Yes,' said Archie. 'I think they're all right – they're in the car – but someone ought to dig them out before they run out of air and die.'

The policeman didn't move for a bit, then suddenly turned and started running down the hill, calling into his radio for backup while he ran. Both the women ran after him, and Archie was left with the man in the brown overalls.

'So . . . is my piano under there as well?' he asked, hopefully.

'No,' said Archie, 'I think you'll find your piano is in there.' He pointed to the house across the road.

The man frowned. 'Why would it be in there?'

Archie thought about this.

'I have no idea,' he said, eventually. 'No idea at all.'

The policeman asked Archie to wait while they sorted everything out, and sorting everything out seemed to take quite a long time. An hour later, Archie was still waiting, sitting on a wall, when Cyd, the girl from the car, came over to join him.

'I wanted to thank you,' she said, 'for calling the police and getting them to dig us out. I might still be stuck in there if you hadn't.'

'That's all right,' said Archie.

Cyd sat down on the wall beside him.

'They've worked out what happened with the piano,' she said. 'It was really weird. The man was supposed to deliver it to number sixteen, so he stopped at the house at the top of the hill because it had number sixteen on the gate. Only it wasn't really number sixteen. It was number ninety-one, but the house number had swung upside down. Then, while they were trying to sort it out, the piano rolled down the hill, and it stopped outside the real number sixteen and they took it inside. Can

you believe it? I can't. I mean . . . all those things happening. If I hadn't seen it, I'd never have believed it.'

'No,' said Archie. 'People usually don't.'

Cyd looked at him. 'You mean . . . things like this have happened to you before?'

'They happen to me every day,' said Archie.

'Every day?'

'Pretty much.' Archie nodded.

'Wow!' The girl smiled. 'That must make life interesting. Look, Mum wants to buy you an ice cream or something, you know, to say thank you for saving my life. Would that be all right?'

And Archie said yes, he thought it would be very all right. And after that, the morning turned out to be a lot more cheerful than he had expected. Though his mother was not particularly cheerful when he got home. What was the point, she said, of going out to post a letter, when you came back two hours later with it still in your pocket?

'Honestly!' she muttered as she left the letter on the table in the hall. 'I don't believe it, Archie!'

2. On Tuesday . . .

On Tuesday, when Archie was walking down
to the shops to get some milk, he found a little
dog lying on the pavement.

The dog wasn't moving, and Archie's first
thought was that it might be dead. But he
remembered his father once saying that the
way to tell if an animal was still alive was to put
your fingers on its neck and feel for a pulse.
So he dropped the coat he had been carrying,
knelt down and put his fingers on the dog's
neck. He wasn't quite sure how many fingers
to use or where to put them, so he used all of
them, trying to see if there was any sign of life.

'What are you doing?' said a voice behind him.

Archie looked round and saw a large woman with a gardening fork standing on the other side of the low wall that ran along the pavement.

'You're strangling my sister's dog!' The woman had a look of astonishment on her face. 'I don't believe it! You're strangling Timmy!'

'No!' said Archie. 'I'm not, I . . .' He snatched his hands away from the dog's neck and stepped quickly back from the little body on the pavement. Unfortunately, the Velcro strip on one of his trainers had got caught in the dog's collar and, as he moved his foot away, the dog moved with it. In fact, it sailed through the air before breaking free from the strap on Archie's shoe and landing with a *thud* against the trunk of a tree.

'You kicked him!' said the large woman,

her look of astonishment changing to one of horror. 'First you strangle him and then you

kick him into a tree. I don't believe it!'

'No, no!' said Archie. 'That just . . . happened.' He ran over to where the dog was lying on the pavement and picked it up. The little body lay in his hands, very still.

'You've killed him, haven't you!' said the woman.

Archie opened his mouth to explain but, before he could speak, a small, rather sharp woman appeared from round the side of the house.

'What's going on?' she demanded as she hurried towards them. 'What's happened?'

'This boy,' said the large woman, 'has killed Timmy!' She pointed to Archie. 'He strangled him with his bare hands, then kicked him into that tree. I saw him do it!'

The small woman stared at Archie and at the dog he was holding, her mouth open in disbelief.

'That's not true,' said Archie. 'I didn't kick him anywhere. Well, not on purpose.' He stepped forward and carefully placed the body of the dog on the wall. 'It was . . . an accident.'

'An accident!' The large woman snorted. 'How do you kick a dog to death by accident?' She turned to her sister. 'He did it on purpose. I saw him do it!'

The small woman did not answer. Instead, her lip quivering, her eyes filling with tears, she gazed down at the body of her dog, and began to cry.

'He's gone!' she sobbed. 'My little Timmy . . . gone!'

'Look, I'm really sorry,' said Archie, 'but if you'd just let me explain—'

'I think you've done quite enough for one

day,' said the large woman, putting an arm round her sister. 'We'd like you to go now.'

Archie tried twice to tell the women the truth, but each time it only seemed to make things worse and, in the end, he did as he was told. He picked up his coat from where he'd left it on the pavement and walked sadly away.

Behind him, he could hear the large woman telling the small one that they would bury the body together, perhaps under the lilac bush that little Timmy had loved so much when he was alive, and then . . .

'*Aaaaaaaagh!*'

Archie turned round.

'What's happened?' The small woman had stopped crying for a moment and was staring down at the garden wall. 'Where is he? Where's he gone?'

Both women were staring at the place on the wall where Archie had left the dog. They looked at the wall, then down at the pavement, then at the garden on the other side, but there was no sign of the dog. It had disappeared.

The large woman stared accusingly at

Archie. 'What have you done with him?' she
demanded.

'Me?' said Archie. 'I haven't done anything!'

'You've stolen his body, haven't you!' said
the small woman.

'No!' said Archie. 'Of course I haven't! Why
would I steal a dog's body?'

'He probably wants to do experiments on
it,' said the large woman, her eyes narrowing
as she stared at Archie. 'I've read about

children like him.'

Archie wondered how much worse this whole business could get.

'Look,' he said, firmly. 'I haven't stolen your dog's body. How could I? I mean, where would I have put it?' He was wearing jeans and a T-shirt, and held out his arms to show there was nothing there.

'He's got it in his coat,' said the small woman. She pointed. 'Look! You can see he's got it in his pocket.' There was indeed a bulge in the pocket of the coat he was carrying, but Archie assured the women that there was nothing inside.

'It's empty,' he said. 'I'll show you, if you like.' And he reached into the

pocket of his coat and took out . . . the body of
the little dog.

'How *could* you!' The large woman shook
her head in disbelief. 'First you kill him, and
then, when all we want to do is bury him
quietly in the garden, you steal his body! I
don't *believe* it!'

'Let's give him a taste of his own medicine,'
said the small woman, who had stopped crying
and was looking at Archie as if she was quite
in the mood to do some killing herself. She
began rolling up the sleeves of her
blouse.

'Let's see how *he* likes
being strangled
and kicked, shall
we . . . ?'

'Please,' said Archie, backing away. 'Please! I have no idea how that body got into my pocket and—'

'I do,' said a voice.

Archie spun round to find a girl standing on the pavement behind him. He recognized her at once. It was Cyd, the girl he had met the day before in the car that got buried under a lorry-load of gravel.

'I live over there,' said Cyd, pointing to a house on the other side of the road, 'and I saw everything that happened.'

'You mean you saw this boy strangle Timmy, and then come back and steal his body?' said the small woman.

'No,' said Cyd, 'because that's not what happened.' She took a deep breath. 'What happened was that you . . .' – she pointed to the large woman – '. . .were out in front of your house doing some gardening, and the dog was chewing at the buttons on your shoe.'

'Oh, yes!' The large woman gave a sad smile. 'Timmy loved doing that!'

'And then one of the buttons came off,' Cyd continued, 'and got stuck in his throat, so that he couldn't breathe. You didn't notice that he was choking, and you didn't see him stagger out on to the pavement and collapse. This boy found him, bent down to try and help . . .'

'Yes!' said Archie, vigorously. 'Yes, that's right!'

Cyd ignored him, and continued talking to the large woman. 'But then you told him to get away, so he kicked the dog into the tree.'

'No!' said Archie. 'No, that's not right at all!'

'And it's very lucky for you that he did,' said Cyd, still ignoring Archie, 'because that is what

29

saved the dog's life.'

There was a pause. The two women looked rather confused.

'But he didn't save Timmy's life!' said the large woman eventually. 'Timmy's dead!'

'No, he's not,' said Cyd. 'You see, hitting the tree dislodged the button from his throat. It knocked him out, but it meant he could breathe again.' As she spoke, she held up a small brown button. 'I just found this on the pavement.'

The large woman looked at the button and then at her shoes, which had one button missing.

'I . . . I don't understand,' she said.

'Nor do I,' said Archie.

'You . . . you think Timmy's still alive?' said the small woman doubtfully. 'Really?'

'Well, he was two minutes ago,' said Cyd. She turned to Archie. 'After you left him on the wall, I could see him starting to move. You were all so busy talking to each other you didn't notice, but I saw him trying to stand up, and then he fell off the wall. Luckily, he landed on your coat, but you didn't see that either. Then, when you picked your coat up, he slid down into the pocket. Which is where you found him.'

There was another long pause while the others absorbed this information.

Archie stared at the dog in his hand.

'He doesn't look very alive,' he said, but at just that moment, the little dog slowly opened one eye and stared up at him.

'He's *not* dead!' shouted the small woman. She leaped over the wall, rushed over to Archie and scooped the dog up in her hands. 'I don't believe it! Timmy, you're still alive!' She held the little dog up to her face and it began licking her cheek.

'Yes, he's alive,' said Cyd. 'Thanks to Archie. He saved your dog's life. In fact, he saved it twice.'

'Twice?' The small woman looked at her, puzzled, the dog still clutched to her face.

'He saved it once when he got the button out of its throat,' said Cyd, 'and then again when he stopped you from burying it while it was still alive.'

'Oh, yes! Yes, he did, didn't he! Oh, I don't believe how stupid I've been!' The small woman had started crying again, but she was smiling gratefully at Archie through her tears.

'You saved little Timmy!' The large woman had come over to stand beside her sister. 'And all I did was shout at you. I am *so* sorry!'

Both women told Archie how sorry they were several times, and then they insisted that the children come indoors for some cake and a glass of milk. They were still saying how sorry they were, and how grateful, half an hour later, when Archie finally said that he really ought to be going. Before he left, the large woman took a ten pound note from her pocket and insisted that he take it as a small reward for what he had done, and the short woman gave Cyd a box of chocolates.

'I am *really* glad you turned up when you did,' said Archie, when he and Cyd were standing back out on the pavement. 'I was starting to get a bit worried.'

'I'm glad I could help,' said Cyd. 'Especially after what you did for me, yesterday.' She paused. 'You know, when you told me odd things happened to you every day, I didn't really believe you.'

'No,' said Archie. 'People don't usually.'

'But they really do, don't they?'

'Oh, yes,' said Archie. 'Every day.'

'Do you know why?'

'Not really.' Archie gave a little shrug. 'Dad says it's the Laws of Chance. He says odd things happen to most people at some time in their lives, but they're not evenly spread out. Some people have a few odd things happen to them, some people don't have anything happen at all, and some people have odd things happen to them every day.'

'Like you?' said Cyd.

'Yes,' Archie nodded. 'Like me.'

'So . . .' said Cyd thoughtfully, 'you think something odd might happen to you tomorrow?'

'Probably,' said Archie. 'If I go out.'

'Well, if you *do* go out,' said Cyd, 'could I come along and watch? You could pick me up on the way to wherever you're going.'

'All right,' said Archie. 'If you like.'

'Good!' Cyd tucked her box of chocolates under her arm. 'I'll see you tomorrow then.' She turned, crossed the road and, before she let herself into her house, gave Archie a wave and smiled.

She had, Archie noticed, a nice smile.

His mother, however, was definitely not smiling when he got home.

'How can anyone,' she demanded, 'take an *hour* to walk down to the shops for some milk, and then come back without any? Honestly!' She let out a long, exasperated sigh. 'I don't believe it, Archie!'

3. On Wednesday . . .

On Wednesday, Archie went down to the library to change some books.

On his way, he called in at Cyd's house, as he had promised, to ask if she would like to come too, and Cyd said yes please. She was going on holiday to Florida at the end of the week and wanted something to read on the plane.

As they walked down the hill together, Cyd asked Archie what sort of odd things had happened to him in the past.

Archie told her the story of the time a small alligator had fallen out of the sky and landed in the hood of his coat. And about the time

he had been digging in a friend's garden and
found a cluster of World War Two bombs and,
when they got to the library, he was in the
middle of telling her about the time he had
been trapped in a lift with a woman giving
birth to twins.

'They were telling me what to do, on
the emergency phone,' he said, 'but then I
found . . .' He paused. 'My hand's stuck!'

'That must have been embarrassing,' said
Cyd. 'What did you do?'

'No, no, I mean . . . now,' said Archie. 'My
hand's stuck now.'

There were double doors at the entrance
to the library, each with a brass handle in the
middle. Archie had used his left hand to take
the handle of the door on the left, only to find
that the door didn't move. So he had taken the
handle of the door on the right with his right
hand, pushed it open, and was about to walk
in when he found his left hand was stuck to
the other door.

'How do you mean, it's stuck?' asked Cyd.

'I mean it's stuck!' said Archie. 'As in *it won't move*.' He paused. 'I don't believe it! This one's stuck as well!'

Archie had tried to move his right hand from the right door handle, and found that that one didn't move either.

Looking through the glass at the top of the doors, Archie could see an old lady hurrying towards them from inside the building, calling anxiously.

'What's she saying?' he asked.

'I think she's telling you not to touch the door handles,' said Cyd, 'because they've got glue on them.'

The old lady pulled open one of the double doors. Archie's hand went with it.

'You don't want to touch the handles,' she said. 'I've just put glue on them!'

'Thank you,' said Archie. 'Useful information but . . . a little late.'

'Oh, dear!' said the old lady. 'Are you stuck?'

'Yes,' said Archie. 'Yes, I am.'

'I'm *so* sorry.' The old lady looked at Archie apologetically. 'The glue was for me, you see. But then I thought, before I stuck myself on, that it might be a good idea to make one last trip to the toilet.'

'You were going to glue yourself to the door handles?' said Cyd.

The old lady nodded. 'I was going to chain myself to them originally,' she said, 'but the man at the shop said superglue would be cheaper. Steel chain is quite expensive you see, and of course I'd have to buy some padlocks as well. The man said, if I just glued myself to the door handles, they'd never get me free. Not without pulling my hands off.'

'Did he?' Archie sighed. 'Oh, good . . .'

'Forgive my asking,' said Cyd, 'but why would anyone want to glue themselves to the doors of a library?'

'It's a protest!' said the old lady. 'Like it says on the banner!'

'What banner?' asked Cyd.

'Don't tell me it's fallen down again!' said the old lady. 'It must be this wind. Excuse me.'

Getting out of the library with Archie glued

to the doors was a little tricky. The old lady tried hitching up her skirt and stepping over his arms, but she was not very tall and, in the end, she went down on all fours and crawled underneath.

Outside, she found the edge of the banner that had blown down and got Cyd to hold it in place. Then, while she pinned it back up, the old lady explained that someone was planning to pull down the library and build a car park.

'I'm sure he hasn't got proper permission,' she said, 'and I'm not going to let it happen.' She pointed to a poster on one of the doors. 'Lots of people use this library, and I've told him if he tries to knock this place down I'm quite happy to be buried in the rubble.'

When she had finished putting up the banner, she came back to stand beside Archie. 'I'll just take some of my clothes off,' she said, 'and then I'll glue myself beside you.'

Archie looked rather alarmed. 'Take some clothes off? Why?'

'Well, I can't do it *after* I've glued myself to the doors, can I?' said the old lady. 'I'd never be able to pull the sleeves down.'

'I think Archie was wondering,' said Cyd, 'why you wanted to take your clothes off in the first place.'

'Oh, I see!' The old lady smiled. 'Well, that's for the reporters, you see. My granddaughter says the newspapers love taking pictures of women with not many clothes on.'

She began to unbutton her cardigan.

'I'm not sure getting undressed is a good idea,' said Cyd. 'There's a very chilly wind . . .'

'We all have to make sacrifices,' said the old lady cheerfully. But then a worried look crossed her face. 'Although, maybe I should visit the toilet again first. Just to be on the safe side.'

'You don't have to worry,' Cyd told Archie when the old lady had gone back into the library. 'I can get you free.'

'You can?' said Archie. 'How?'

'There's a solvent you can use to get rid of glue,' said Cyd. 'My mum's a nurse – she does that sort of thing all the time.' She had taken out her mobile and was tapping in the numbers. 'I'll just call her and tell her what's happened.'

Archie was about to say thank you when he noticed a man with a pointy nose and a shiny suit standing a few feet away, looking very cross.

'What's going on here?' he demanded.

'Well . . .' said Archie.

The man with the pointy nose gestured to the banner overhead and the posters on the wall.

'A protest?' he said. 'You're protesting about me knocking down the library?'

'Well . . .' said Archie.

'Don't be so stupid!' said the man. 'Come on. Move!'

'I can't,' said Archie. 'I—'

'I think you can!' said the man with the pointy nose, and he grabbed one of Archie's arms and pulled.

'*Ow!*' said Archie.

'You can't just pull him,' said Cyd. 'He's glued to the doors. You'll tear all his skin off.'

'I don't care,' said the man with the pointy nose. 'I don't mind how much skin I tear off. And if pulling him doesn't work, I'll get a knife and cut off his hands.' He pulled again.

'*Eeow!*' said Archie.

'Help!' said Cyd in a loud voice. 'Somebody help, please!'

'What's going on here, then?' A burly-looking man had stopped on the pavement.

'It's nothing,' said the man with the pointy nose. 'Just this kid causing trouble.'

'I am not causing trouble,' said Archie.

'This man says he's going to cut off Archie's hands with a knife,' said Cyd.

'No, I didn't!' said the man with the pointy nose.

'Yes, you did,' said Cyd.

'Well, all right, I did, but it was just a joke!'

'*I have glued myself to the doors . . .*' – the burly man had begun reading from one of the posters on the door beside Archie – '*. . . to stop them knocking down the library.*' He turned to the man with the pointy nose. 'I didn't know anyone was knocking down the library.'

'Someone's knocking down the library?' said a woman with a shopping trolley who happened to be passing. 'Who's knocking down the library?' She turned to her companion. 'Did you know anything about them knocking down the library?'

Archie was never quite sure where all the people came from but a crowd gathered on the pavement with remarkable speed. Ten minutes later there were at least fifty people there, all asking the same questions. Who was knocking down the library? Did they have permission? Why hadn't anyone been told?

And there was a good deal of murmured support for the young boy who had glued himself to the door handles in protest.

You had to admire him for sticking to his principles, someone said. It was better than being at home glued to the television. And when they read the words on the poster that said 'I am prepared to die in the rubble rather than let this library be destroyed', a lot of people told Archie they thought he was very brave.

A lot of people also wanted to know who was pulling down the library and why, and Cyd told them that the man with the pointy nose was the one who was doing it.

The man with the pointy nose tried to explain that he was only pulling down the

library because it really was the best thing to do.

'What we need in this area,' he said, 'is more parking spaces, not a library. There's already a huge library in the centre of town – and who wants this one? I mean, nobody actually uses it, do they?'

'I do,' said Archie. 'So does Cyd.'

'Right!' The man with the pointy nose laughed. 'So a few kids come down—'

'There's a reading group that meets here every Thursday,' said Cyd, who had been studying one of the posters.

'OK, so there's a reading group—'

'And the Mums and Toddlers meet on Mondays,' added Cyd.

'So a few Mums and Toddlers come down here as well—'

'And the Chess Club meets here,' said Cyd, 'and the Over-Sixties Murder Mystery

Society and the—'

'All right!' The man with the pointy nose held up his hands. 'But apart from a few kids, a reading group, the Mums and Toddlers, the Chess Club and the Over-Sixties Murder Mystery Society . . . does anyone actually use this library?'

'Yes,' said the burly man from the front of the crowd, 'I do. So does my wife. And you're

not knocking it down. Not while I'm here.'
And he came and stood beside Archie. 'I'm
with the kid.'

'Me too,' said a voice.

'And me!' said another. And the crowd
swept forward until they were all standing in a
great circle in front of Archie.

The man with the pointy nose looked as
if he was about to say something, but then
changed his mind.

'I don't believe it,' he muttered. 'All right,
I give up. You can keep your stupid library!'
and he stomped off.

Watching him go, everyone started cheering.

'Where did all these people come from?' asked the old lady, peering over Archie through the gap in the doors.

'They came to support the protest,' Archie told her.

'Really?' The old lady looked pleased. 'I'd better hurry up and take my clothes off then . . .'

'I don't think that'll be necessary,' said Cyd. 'Not now. Not ever. I think your library's been saved.'

'I don't believe it!' The old lady beamed with pleasure. 'Has it really?'

Soon after, when Cyd's mother had arrived and unglued Archie from the door handles, there was more cheering from the crowd, and they were still singing 'For he's a jolly good fellow' as he began walking home.

'I still can't believe it,' said Cyd as she walked beside him. 'Yesterday it was the dog, the day before that the piano, and today . . . you save a library! It's amazing, isn't it!'

'Yes,' said Archie. 'I suppose it is.'

'I mean, something odd really does happen to you every day, doesn't it?'

'Yes,' said Archie.

'Your life is just so . . . *exciting*, isn't it!'

'Oh, yes,' said Archie. 'Very exciting.'

He did not say so, but there were times when he would have preferred life to be rather *less* exciting. But, he thought, if you did have to find yourself glued to the library doors with a man threatening to cut your hands off, it was a lot better to do it with someone like Cyd beside you, calling for help and getting people to come and unglue you.

'If you're going anywhere tomorrow,' said Cyd, 'can I come with you?'

'Definitely,' said Archie. 'I'd like that.'

And Cyd looked rather pleased.

Archie's mother, however, was not at all pleased when he got home. How anyone could spend two hours down at the library and come back at the end of it with exactly the same books was, she said, beyond her.

'Honestly,' she muttered as she strode off to the kitchen. 'I don't believe it, Archie!'

4. On Thursday . . .

On Thursday, Archie had arranged to meet Cyd by the lake in the park. Cyd had told him she needed to go into town first, to buy a new swimming costume for when she went on holiday, and Archie said he would wait for her by the lake.

He had set off with a bag containing a Frisbee, two tennis rackets and some balls, but, when he got to the lake, all those things were gone and instead his bag was full of neatly-bundled piles of fifty-pound notes.

When Cyd arrived, Archie showed her the

money and she worked out that, as there were a hundred notes in each bundle, and fifty bundles altogether, this meant there was a total of a quarter of a million pounds.

'Why would anyone put a quarter of a million pounds in my bag?' said Archie. 'And what have they done with my Frisbee?'

'Are you sure it *is* your bag?' said Cyd. 'I know it looks like your bag, but . . . did you put it down or anything on your way here?'

And Archie remembered that he had put his bag down on a bench, when he arrived at the park, so he could have a drink at the water fountain.

Thinking about it, he also remembered that the bag had not been on the bench when he picked it up, but underneath.

'I reckon,' said Cyd, 'someone's taken your bag by mistake and left theirs behind.' She looked around the park. 'They're probably looking for it right now.'

They probably were, Archie thought. If he

had lost a quarter of a million pounds
by picking up the wrong bag, he would
definitely be looking for the right one.

'How about,' said Cyd, 'we walk round and
see if there's anyone with a bag like yours? If
you go that way, and I go this way . . .' – she
pointed in the two directions – '. . . and we
meet over there by the main gates, one of us is
bound to see them.'

Archie agreed. They both set off, and he
was about halfway to the gates when a tall man
in a dark suit came running towards him.

'Archie?' the man called. 'Archie,
are you all right?'

'I'm fine, thank you,' said
Archie politely. 'Who are you?'

'I'm Rawlings,' said the tall man. 'Head of
Security. I'm in charge of making sure you get
home safely.'

While he was speaking, the man had been
tapping at a phone which he now held to his
face. 'It's OK,' he said. 'I've found him . . . He

says he's fine . . . Yes, yes, of course . . .' He held out the phone to Archie. 'Your mother wants to talk to you,' he said.

Archie took the phone.

'Mum?'

'Oh, Archie!' The voice on the other end was sobbing with relief. 'It's so wonderful to hear you. Are you *sure* you're all right?'

'I'm fine . . .' said Archie. 'But—'

'I'm on my way to get you!' the voice interrupted. 'We should be there in a minute or so. Stay with Mr Rawlings. He'll keep you safe. Oh, darling, I'm so happy!'

It was good to know the

woman on the other end of the phone was happy, Archie thought, but he couldn't help wondering who she was. She certainly wasn't his mother. But before he could say anything she had hung up.

'I'm a bit confused,' he said, as he handed the phone back to the tall man. 'That woman wasn't—'

'Don't worry about it!' The tall man patted Archie reassuringly on the shoulder. 'Things are bound to seem a bit strange at first. The important thing is that you're safe!' He knelt down so that his face was on a level with Archie's. 'But if there's anything you can tell us, anything you can remember, we really need to know.'

'About what?' asked Archie.

'About where you've been, where they took you, how many men there were – everything that's happened since you were kidnapped.' The tall man smiled, encouragingly.

'I was kidnapped?' said Archie.

The tall man gave him an odd look. 'On Friday. You don't remember?'

'No,' said Archie. 'No, I don't.' And he had begun to say the man must be confusing him with someone else when his words were drowned out by the noise of a helicopter hovering overhead. It was flying very low, and, to Archie's surprise, it actually landed on the grass right in front of them.

The tall man wasn't surprised at all. In fact, he waved to the pilot and then at a woman in a smart pink skirt who was climbing out the door and running, as fast as she could, towards Archie.

'Oh, Archie!' She swept him up in her arms and held him very close. 'Thank goodness

we've found you!' She pulled away and held
Archie at arm's length. 'You poor boy! Look
at these awful clothes they've made you wear!'
She turned to the tall man. 'You're sure they
didn't hurt him? What's he told you?'

'Nothing yet,' said the tall man. 'He says he
can't remember.'

'He can't remember?'

'They probably drugged him.' Another

man had climbed out of the helicopter and was standing beside the woman. He had a doctor's bag with him that he placed on the ground before stepping in front of Archie.

'Now, let's have a look at you,' he said.

Archie backed away.

'It's all right, darling!' said the woman, soothingly. 'He's not going to hurt you. This is Doctor Matthews, remember?'

'No, I don't remember,' said Archie. 'I don't remember any of you, because I've never seen any of you before in my life.'

The people around him all looked rather startled, and the woman looked particularly upset. 'Oh, Archie,' she said sadly. 'What have they done to you?'

'Nobody's done anything to me,' said Archie, 'because I am not your son and I

have not been kidnapped. My name is Archie
Coates. I live in Garfield Crescent, and I came
to the park this morning to play Frisbee with a
friend.'

'It's probably the shock,' said the doctor,
thoughtfully. 'It's upset his mind and he's
blanked out everything that happened. I'll
give him something to calm him down.' He
reached into his bag and took out a syringe.

Archie's father had always told him it was
important to do whatever the doctor said, but
he really didn't like the idea of being given
an injection by someone he didn't know.
However, when he tried to run away he found
himself firmly in the grip of the tall man.

'It's all right, Archie,' the man was saying.
'You'll feel much better in a minute . . .'

At the last moment, to his great relief,
Archie saw Cyd coming across the grass
towards him.

'Cyd!' he said. 'Could you tell these people
who I am? The woman thinks I'm her son and

I've been kidnapped, and she wants the doctor to give me an injection so she can take me away in her helicopter.'

'Ah!' Cyd nodded. 'I thought it must be something like that!' She turned to the woman. 'I'm sorry,' she said, 'but this is not your son.'

'Yes, it is!' The woman put her arms round Archie's shoulders and pulled him close. 'You think I wouldn't recognize my own child?'

'I know he *looks* like your son,' said Cyd, 'but this is Archie Coates. He lives at thirteen Garfield Crescent. With his mother and father.'

'I . . . I don't believe it!' said the woman, still holding on to Archie.

'The person you're looking for,' continued Cyd, 'is sitting over there.' She pointed over to the far side of the park where a sad little figure could be seen, with his back to them, slumped on a bench. 'He's a bit dazed. I think he may have been drugged.'

The tall man was running across the grass
even before Cyd had finished talking, and the
woman was right behind him.

'He looks just like you,' said Cyd to Archie,
'except for the clothes. In fact, I thought he
was you at first. But when I said "hi", he didn't
know who I was. He said he'd been told to
wait on the bench until someone came to pick

him up. Then I saw all the fuss going on here and came over.'

A moment later, the woman and the tall man were walking back towards them with a boy who looked *exactly* like Archie. It was, Archie thought, a bit like looking in a mirror. The other Archie was the same height, had the same face, even the same shaped ears.

'I'm so sorry,' said the woman in the pink trouser suit. 'You must have thought we were mad . . .'

'That's all right,' said Archie. 'No harm done.'

'Could I ask,' said Cyd, 'if you had to pay a ransom to get your son back?'

'I did,' said the woman in the smart pink skirt. 'But it doesn't matter. Nothing matters as long as Archie's all right.'

'Was the ransom,' said Cyd, 'supposed to be left in a black bag on a bench by the water fountain over there? And was it, by any chance, a quarter of a million pounds?'

'Yes! Yes, it was!' The woman looked at Cyd in astonishment. 'But how could you possibly know that?'

'Show them, Archie,' said Cyd.

And Archie took the bag from his back and opened the top to reveal the neatly-piled stacks of fifty-pound notes.

Everyone stared at the money.

'I don't believe it!' said the woman.

It was almost an hour before the woman, the doctor and the other Archie took off in the helicopter.

The woman tried to get Archie to keep one of the bundles of fifty-pound notes as a reward, but he said he wouldn't, thank you, as he hadn't really done anything. The woman did, however, insist on sending the tall man into town to get a replacement bag, a new

Frisbee and two new tennis rackets and balls for him. Then, before she left, she gave him a card with her telephone number on it.

'If there's ever anything I can do for you,' she said, 'anything at all, you call that number, all right?'

Cyd and Archie watched the helicopter disappear into the sky with a roar of noise and wind.

'Well!' said Cyd, when it had gone. 'You come to the park for a game of Frisbee, find a bag full of money, get mistaken for someone who's been kidnapped, a helicopter comes to take you away . . . I mean, how cool is all that!' She stopped. 'Where are you going?'

'I'm going home,' said Archie, heading towards the park entrance, 'before anything else happens.'

He did not say so, but he had found being grabbed in the park by people he didn't know who wanted to give him an injection and take him away in a helicopter was quite enough excitement for one day.

So he and Cyd walked home and spent the rest of the afternoon up in Archie's room playing draughts.

Archie's mother couldn't understand it.

'How can you stay indoors on a lovely, sunny day like this,' she said, 'when you could be outside playing in the park? Honestly, Archie! I don't believe it!'

5. On Friday . . .

On Friday, Archie's mother asked if he would mind going out to look for the toy lion his little sister had lost.

'It's her favourite toy,' she said, 'and we can't find it anywhere. She must have dropped it when we went down to the shops this morning. Could you go and look?'

Archie said he would, and he called in at Cyd's house on the way to ask if she would help. Cyd agreed – and in fact she was the one who first saw the missing lion. It was in a bush in the garden of a large house in Wigmore Street.

'Your sister must have thrown it out of her

buggy,' she said, and she was about to jump over the wall to get it when Archie held her back.

'I think we should ask permission first,' he said. His father had told him you should always ask permission before you went into someone else's garden.

So the two of them walked up the path, and knocked on the front door. It was answered by an elderly man with a bald head.

'I'm sorry to bother you,' said Archie politely, 'but there's a lion in your garden and I wondered—'

'A lion!' The old man looked rather alarmed. 'Are you sure?'

'It's in that bush,' said Cyd, pointing across the grass. 'We could see it from the pavement and we thought—'

'I don't believe it!' muttered the old man. 'All right! Inside, both of you. Come on! Quick as you can!' And before Archie could speak, he had pulled both children into the house and slammed the door.

'You!' The old man pointed to Cyd. 'Call the police and tell them what you saw. Say it's an emergency!' As he spoke, he was fumbling with a holster hanging on the coat rack, and taking out what looked like a gun.

'I don't think we need to call the police,' said Cyd. 'It's not a real lion and—'

'I know,' said the old man briskly. 'Technically, it's a cougar. But it can still be

dangerous. Now,
please. Do as
I say!'

'No,' said
Archie firmly.
'She is not calling
the police because
of a toy that my
sister threw out

of her buggy. All we need is
permission to go in your garden and get
it back.'

The old man looked at him. 'A toy?'

'Yes,' said Archie. 'It's a toy lion. Called
Bingo.' He was beginning to wish he had let
Cyd jump over the wall and just take it.

'Wait here!' The old man crossed the hall,
opened a door leading off to the right and
peered cautiously inside. A moment later, he
closed the door and turned to the children
with a huge smile of relief. 'You're quite right!
Panic over. He's still in there!'

'You . . . you mean you have a *real* lion in the house?' asked Cyd.

'I know we're not supposed to.' The old man looked rather embarrassed. 'It was an emergency, you see. Kevin had to put him somewhere while . . .' He stopped and stared at the door on the opposite side of the hall. 'Oh, no!' His voice dropped to a whisper. 'I don't believe it!'

'What?' asked Archie. 'What is it?'

The door on the left side of the hall stood slightly open and the children watched as the old man walked across, put his head round and looked inside.

'She's gone!' He turned to face the children, and flung open the door. 'Look! She's not here!'

With the door wide open, the children could see that, apart from a dining table and some chairs, the room was indeed quite empty.

'Who's not here?' asked Archie.

'The leopard!' said the old man. He looked

nervously round the hall.

'You have a leopard in your house as well as a lion?' said Cyd.

'If she's got out,' muttered the old man, 'we could be in real trouble!' He was backing into the dining room as he spoke. 'You'd better come in here with me.'

'Why?' asked Archie.

'Because there's a leopard somewhere in the house,' said the old man, 'and this is the one place I know it *isn't*.'

Archie was about to say that the only place he was going was back outside, when he saw a leopard standing at the top of the stairs. It was making a sort of rasping noise as it breathed. You might have thought it was purring if you didn't know that leopards don't purr.

'Let's get into the dining room, Archie,' said Cyd, and, moving very quickly, they both stepped inside and the old man closed the door.

'What do we do now?' asked Archie.

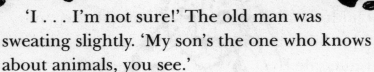

'I . . . I'm not sure!' The old man was sweating slightly. 'My son's the one who knows about animals, you see.'

'And where's he?' asked Cyd.

'He's gone down to the garage to get the van.' The old man mopped at his face with a handkerchief. 'He said he'd only be a few minutes. We just have to wait till he gets back.'

'What's going on here?' asked Archie sternly. 'What are you doing with a lion and a leopard in your house?'

The old man let out a long sigh and sat down in one of the chairs. 'I know it must seem odd,' he said, 'but my son works for a wildlife park in Dorset. They sent him to Leeds to pick up a lion and a leopard from a zoo there, and on his way back he had some engine trouble. Of course, he couldn't take the van to the garage with two wild animals in the back, so he left them here with me while he took the van in for repair. It was only for an hour, you see.' He looked appealingly at the

children. 'I'm really sorry about all this, but I promise, as long as you stay in here, you're quite safe.'

'Are you sure about that?' said Cyd.

'Oh, yes!' The old man nodded reassuringly. 'It's a very solid door. There's no way it can get in!'

'It got out,' said Cyd. 'Probably by pushing down that door handle with its paw. And if it got out, I don't see why it couldn't get back in.'

The old man looked at Cyd and then at the door handle.

'You're right!' He stood up hurriedly. 'I'll put a chair under the handle so that—'

He stopped. Looking towards the door, they could all see the handle was already moving downwards. There was a quiet *click* and the door swung open to reveal the leopard lowering its paw before padding quietly into the room.

'Don't panic!' The old man pushed the children behind him. 'Kevin showed me how

to use this . . .' – he was holding the gun in his right hand as he spoke – '. . . it fires a dart that'll put it to sleep. If I can just find the safety catch . . .'

There were several tense seconds as he fiddled with the gun while the leopard moved steadily closer, and then there was a loud bang.

The leopard gave a start and shrank back, making a hissing sound.

'Did you hit it?' asked Cyd.

'I'm afraid not . . .' The old man was swaying slightly as he spoke. He looked down at the dart sticking out of his foot. 'Oh, dear,' he said. 'Oh, dear, oh,

dear, oh . . .' And he crashed, face down, onto the floor.

The leopard moved cautiously forward, sniffed briefly at the body, then lifted its head and began moving towards the children.

'I don't believe it!' A young man in shirt sleeves had appeared in the doorway. 'What is going on in here?'

At the sound of his voice, the leopard turned and ran towards him, pushing its nose against his leg. The young man bent down and grabbed it by the scruff of the neck. 'Come on you!' he said. 'Out. Now!' And he pushed the leopard into the hall and closed the door before kneeling down beside the body of the old man.

'Would someone,' he said, pulling the dart out of the old man's foot, 'mind telling me what happened?'

'I don't mind telling you,' said Cyd, 'but you're never going to believe it!'

On the way home, Cyd said she thought it had been very nice of Archie not to report Kevin or his father to the police.

'If you did report them,' she said, 'I think they'd both be in a lot of trouble.'

'I try not to call the police when things happen to me,' Archie told her. 'If I do, it means spending hours describing what happened and then more hours waiting while they write it down. If I did that every day, there'd never be time to do anything else.'

'No,' said Cyd, 'I suppose not.'

'Usually,' Archie went on, 'I don't even tell my parents. But I hope you weren't too frightened or anything.' He looked across at Cyd. 'I'm used to things like that happening, but it can be quite upsetting if you're not. Are you sure you're OK?'

'I'm fine,' said Cyd. 'Just fine.'

She didn't look like someone who'd been frightened or upset, Archie thought. In fact, he was pleased to notice, she looked as if she'd thoroughly enjoyed the whole adventure.

His mother, however, was not at all pleased when he got home.

'You are telling me,' she said crossly, 'that you saw Lucy's lion in somebody's garden but forgot to pick it up and bring it back with you?'

She shook her head. 'Honestly, Archie. I don't believe it!'

6. On Saturday . . .

On Saturday, Archie and Cyd went into town
to watch a bank robbery. It wasn't a real bank
robbery of course. Cyd's mother had heard
from a friend that they were making a film of
a robbery that morning, and Archie and Cyd
decided to go and watch.

They were a little later than they meant
to be. Archie wanted to take some pictures
and had borrowed his mother's camera, but
first they had to find new batteries for it, and
then she had to give him a lesson on how it
worked, and both these things took longer
than expected. Cyd was luckier. She could

take pictures on her phone, and was looking forward to getting some exciting shots.

When they got to the bank, however, there was nothing exciting for them to take pictures of. The street was almost empty.

'I don't believe it!' said Archie. 'Your mum said there'd be hundreds of people here! Where is everyone?'

'I wonder,' said Cyd, 'if we've come to the wrong bank.'

'I'll ask,' said Archie. There wasn't much choice about who to ask. The only other person in the street was a man sitting in a car outside a jeweller's shop.

'Excuse me!' Archie tapped on the car window. 'Is this where the robbery's happening?'

The man in the car looked rather startled. 'Robbery?'

'Yes,' said Archie. 'Is this the right place to come and watch?'

'What . . . what do you know about a robbery?' asked the man in the car, glancing nervously up and down the street.

'Well, not much,' said Archie, 'but Cyd's mum has a friend in the police who said they were going to be filming a robbery here today and we thought—'

But Archie never got a chance to say what he thought, because the man in the car suddenly drove off down the road, very fast.

'How rude!' said Archie. 'He drove off while I was still talking!'

'I don't believe it!' A big man, dressed all in black, had appeared on the pavement, pulling off a ski mask. He was carrying a baseball bat and a large black bag. 'Where's he gone?' he demanded.

'If you're looking for the man in the car,'

said Archie, 'he drove off.'

'Drove off? Why?'

'I have no idea,' said Archie. 'All I did was ask him if this was where the robbery was happening and—'

'Robbery?' The man in black lowered his voice and looked anxiously at Archie. 'What do you know about the robbery?'

'Well,' said Archie, 'like I told the other man, Cyd's mum has a friend in the police who said they'd be filming a robbery here today—'

'They're *filming* it?' The man in black took out a handkerchief and mopped nervously at the sweat running down his face.

'I think so,' said Archie. 'We were planning to watch it, but . . .'

He stopped. The man in black had thrust both the bag and bat into Archie's arms and was running off down the road as fast as he could go.

'I don't believe it!' said Archie. 'Why do people keep running away when I'm talking to them?'

Cyd did not answer. She was looking thoughtfully at the jewellery shop behind them, and then at the bag in Archie's arms.

'Archie,' she said, 'I wonder if—'

'Oi! You! Stop right there!'

Archie and Cyd spun round in time to see a middle-aged man in glasses come out of a toy shop on the other side of the road and start running towards them.

'And where do you think you're going with that?' he demanded, pointing at the baseball bat that Archie was holding.

'I wasn't going anywhere,' said Archie. 'I was—'

'That bat does not belong to you!' said the man in the glasses. 'You stole it from my shop!'

'No, I didn't!' said Archie.

'Oh, yes, you did! My wife had just put six

of those bats out on display,' said the man.
'And now there's only five. She says the only
other person in the shop was a boy in a red
T-shirt and—'

'But Archie's not wearing a red T-shirt,'
said Cyd. 'It's orange.'

Archie looked down at his shirt. 'I suppose
you could call it a sort of red,' he said.

'No, you couldn't!' said Cyd. 'It's orange.
It's a completely different colour!'

'The colour,' interrupted the man in
glasses, 'is not important! What's important is
the baseball bat. It's not yours!'

'I know it's not,' said Archie. 'But I didn't
steal it.'

'No? So where did you get it?'

'A man gave it to me,' said Archie. 'Just now. And then he ran off.'

'Oh, yes?' The man in glasses smiled, but it was not a nice smile. 'So I'm supposed to believe that a man gave you a baseball bat that looks exactly like the one that's just gone missing from my shop . . . and then ran away?'

'I know it sounds odd,' said Archie, 'but . . . that's what happened.'

'Well, I don't believe it,' said the man, 'and I doubt if the police will believe it either when they get here.' He reached out and took the bat. 'So I'll look after this until they do, shall I? And you can both . . .'

He stopped. While taking the bat, the man's fingers had pulled open the top of the bag and given him a glimpse of what was inside.

Tucking the bat under one arm, he took the bag from Archie, reached in and brought out a fistful of diamond necklaces, strings of pearls and jewel-encrusted bracelets.

'I don't believe it!' said the man. He stared at Archie for several seconds. 'You stole all these as well?'

'I keep telling you,' said Archie. 'I haven't stolen anything!'

'The man who gave him the bat gave him the bag at the same time,' said Cyd.

'You've both been out stealing all morning, haven't you?' The man was still staring at the jewellery in his hand. 'I can't believe it! I mean . . . how old are you?'

Before Archie could reply, however, there came a shout from further down the street.

'Put the bag down! Put the bag down, now! And the bat!'

They turned to see two policemen running down the road towards them. One of them, a sergeant, was holding a spray can. 'Put them down,' he said firmly. 'Unless you want a taste of mace.'

The man with the glasses put down the bat

and the bag, and the police sergeant put him in handcuffs. The other policeman opened up the bag and gave a low whistle at what he saw inside.

'Looks like we got here before he could get away, Sarge!'

The police sergeant looked at the man. 'Care to explain how you come to be in possession of all this jewellery?' he asked.

'I . . . I got it from him,' said the man, pointing to Archie.

'Yes, of course you did,' said the policeman with a grim smile.

'No, no really! *He's* the thief. Him and the girl! They were both in it together,' the man insisted, and he would have said more, but the policeman told him to be quiet.

'You ought to be ashamed of yourself,' said the sergeant, 'trying to put the blame on a couple of kids like that.' And he had just finished putting on the handcuffs when

a woman in a smart skirt and a blue jumper appeared.

'What on earth's going on?' she asked.

'Nothing to be concerned about, madam,' said the policeman. 'This man has just robbed that jewellery shop, but we caught him before he could get away.'

'But that's ridiculous!' said the woman. 'My husband hasn't had time to rob anyone! He was in our shop with me until a minute ago!'

'With you?' The policeman frowned.

'Yes!' The woman pointed. 'We own the toy shop over there.'

'I told you!' said the man with the glasses. 'I came outside because this boy stole a baseball bat from our shop and—'

'Well, he didn't actually steal it, Gavin,' said the woman in blue. 'That's what I came out to tell you.'

'He didn't?'

'No. Nobody stole anything. One of the

bats had fallen down the back of the box, that's all.' She looked at Archie. 'And anyway, I said to look for a boy in a red T-shirt. This one's wearing orange.'

'I think,' said Archie, 'you could say it's a *sort* of red . . .'

'STOP!' said the police sergeant in a very loud voice. 'EVERYBODY! STOP TALKING! NOW!' In the silence that followed, he turned to Archie. 'Did this man come out of that toy shop and find you holding a baseball bat and a bag of jewels?'

'Yes,' said Archie.

'Right.' The policeman looked very stern. 'Would you like to explain how you got them?'

Archie thought for a moment. 'I think I'll let Cyd do the explaining,' he said eventually. 'She's better at this bit than I am.'

Everyone looked at Cyd.

'Well, I *could* explain,' said Cyd, 'but it's probably quicker if you just watch the video.'

She held out her phone. 'I recorded everything that happened, you see.'

The policemen watched the video. It was all there. The man in the car who had driven off, the second man coming out of the jewellers and giving Archie the bag and the bat, and then the man with the glasses running over from the toy shop.

'I recognize the one in the car,' said the police sergeant. 'That's Big Barry Bolan. But I've no idea who the other one is.'

'His name's Fergus,' said Cyd. 'Fergus O'Donnell.'

Both policemen looked at her. 'How do you know that?'

'He dropped his wallet,' Cyd explained, 'when he was getting a handkerchief out of his pocket.' She passed the wallet to the sergeant. 'You'll find his address in there as well.'

'I don't believe it!' said the sergeant.

It was about an hour before everything was sorted out and Archie and Cyd could go home. The police had taken a copy of Cyd's film. The man from the jeweller's shop, who'd been tied up behind the counter, was released and came out to say 'thank you' and to promise them both a reward. And the man with the glasses told both children they should come and choose something from his toy shop, as an apology for the mistake he'd made.

'Well,' said Cyd, as they walked home, 'that was exciting, wasn't it? I think it was even more exciting than the leopard!'

'Yes . . .' Archie sighed. 'I don't know what

I'm going to do when you go on holiday.'

'You'll miss me, will you?' said Cyd.

'I certainly will!' said Archie. 'When things go wrong, it really helps to have someone around who can go and get the glue solvent, or work out that the dog's not dead, or produce a film of what really happened.' He looked at his friend. 'Who's going to do all that when you're away?'

'It's only for a week,' said Cyd. 'And after I get back, I'll be with you every day.'

'You will? Really?'

'It's a promise,' said Cyd, taking his arm,

and for some reason Archie found that a very cheering thought.

What wasn't so cheery was his mother's mood when he got home.

'I don't understand you at all, sometimes,' she said, crossly. 'You make me go to all that trouble this morning to sort out a camera for you, and then you don't take any pictures with it! Honestly! I don't believe it, Archie!'

7. On Sunday . . .

On Sunday, Archie decided to have a quiet day at home.

It had been a busy week and he thought it might be nice if, for one day at least, nothing odd happened to him. It would be particularly nice because, if anything *did* happen, he knew he wouldn't have Cyd to help sort things out because Cyd and her mother had gone to America.

After lunch, Archie's mother asked him to take a pile of magazines to the old lady who lived next door, and he picked up the magazines, opened the front door . . . and

found Cyd standing on the step outside.

'Aren't you supposed to be on holiday?' he said.

'We can't go!' Cyd looked as if she was trying not to cry. 'Mum's had her bag stolen!'

Cyd's mother had been standing on the pavement that morning with their luggage, waiting for the taxi that would take them to the airport, when a young man had run past and snatched her handbag.

'It had our passports and tickets and all our money in it,' said Cyd.

'I don't believe it!' said Archie. 'What are you going to do?'

'I don't know,' said Cyd. 'I didn't know what to do. So I came round here in case, maybe, you could help.'

Archie frowned. 'Me? How?'

'I just thought,' said Cyd, 'if I came round, something might . . . happen.'

Archie let out a long sigh. 'I know odd

things happen to me most days,' he said, 'but I can't *make* them happen. I'm sorry, but if you're thinking I can magically make someone turn up with your mum's missing bag then—'

'Ah, there you are!' said a voice.

Looking down the path, Archie saw the large woman who, on Tuesday, thought he had strangled her sister's dog.

'I've been looking everywhere for you!' she said.

'Me?' asked Archie.

'No, no, not you!' The large woman pointed at Cyd. 'You!' She held up a bag. 'Does this belong to your mother?'

'It's Mum's bag!' said Cyd. 'How did you find Mum's bag?'

'Well,' said the large woman happily, passing the bag across, 'I was out for a walk earlier, when a young man came running down the path and unfortunately tripped over Timmy's lead.' She gestured to the little dog beside her. 'I went to help him up, but he just ran away. Then I noticed he'd dropped that bag, and when I looked inside I realized who it belonged to.'

Cyd was burrowing through the bag's contents. 'It's all here!' she said excitedly. 'The passports, the tickets, the money . . .' She looked up at the large woman. 'Thank you,' she said. 'Thank you very much.'

'Happy to have helped,' said the large woman. 'I owe you both something after what you did for little Timmy.' She looked at her watch. 'Well, I must get on. Have a nice holiday!'

Cyd and Archie went racing round to Cyd's house.

'I think we've still got time,' said Cyd, a little breathlessly, as they ran. 'If Mum can get a taxi and we go straight to the airport,

I think we can still catch the plane.'

But when they got to the house, Cyd's mother wasn't there. Instead, there was a note on the door saying she had gone down to the police station to report the loss of her bag.

Cyd turned to Archie. 'What do we do now?' she asked.

Archie had no idea. They needed to find Cyd's mother and tell her they had the bag but, by the time they found her, it would probably be too late.

'I don't believe it!' said a voice. 'I was just thinking about you two.'

A large green car had drawn up at the pavement, and the man leaning out of the driver's window was the old man with the bald head they had met on Friday at the house with the leopard.

'I wanted to say thank you,' said the old man. 'My son could have been in a lot of trouble if you'd told anyone what happened with the leopard that day. But you kept quiet and I'm very grateful.' He paused. 'You *didn't* tell anyone, did you?'

'No. No, we didn't,' said Cyd.

'Could you give us a lift into town?' asked Archie. 'Only, Cyd needs to find her mother.' He explained about Cyd going on holiday, the

bag with the tickets in it being stolen, and how they had to tell Cyd's mother they had found it, and then get a taxi out to the airport.

'Of course I can give you a lift,' said the old man. 'We'll find your mother and then I'll drive you to the airport myself. It's the least I can do after what you did for me and Kevin. Hop in and buckle up!'

It took a little longer to find Cyd's mother than they expected – she had taken a route round the back of the houses rather than going along the main road – but, when they found her, Cyd gave her the handbag and told her how the old man was prepared to drive them straight to the airport.

Cyd's mother was clearly pleased to have her bag back, but said that, unfortunately, it was too late to catch their flight to Miami.

'If we haven't checked in by two o'clock, they won't let us on the plane,' she said, 'and there's no way we can get to the airport by

then. Not in forty minutes.'

'Your mother's right,' the old man agreed sadly. 'Even a Grand Prix champion couldn't drive you there in forty minutes.'

Cyd looked at Archie. 'There must be *something* we can do!'

'Well,' said Archie, slowly, 'I suppose there is one thing . . .'

The helicopter landed in the field behind
Cyd's house in a gale of dust and noise, and a
tall man in a dark suit stepped out and came
towards Archie with a broad smile on his face.

'Good to see you again, Archie!' he said.
'Mrs Henderson asked me to say she's sorry
she couldn't come herself, but she and the
other Archie are in India.'

'I don't believe it!' Cyd's mum stared in astonishment at the helicopter. 'You're taking us to the airport? Just like that? Why?'

'I'm under strict orders to do anything for Archie and Cyd,' said the tall man. He pointed to the two suitcases. 'Is this all the luggage?'

Three minutes later, they were all strapped

into their seats in the helicopter, and it was lifting off from the field and heading at top speed for the airport.

'It's going to be quite tight,' the tall man told them, shouting above the noise of the engine, 'but we should be OK. The pilot says we'll be landing in thirteen minutes, and then we just have to get to the main terminal so you can check in. I think you'll make it!'

Getting to the main terminal, however,

wasn't quite as easy as the tall man had hoped. He had asked someone to have transport waiting for them but, when they landed at the airport, they found a young man standing on the tarmac with a motorbike.

'I thought it was transport for just one person,' he said apologetically. 'I didn't realize. I'm sorry . . .'

The tall man turned to Cyd and her mother. 'How long before you're supposed to check in?' he asked.

Cyd's mother looked at her watch. 'Four and a half minutes,' she said.

'It'll take at least that long to organize a car,' said the tall man. 'And it's about a mile to the terminal building . . . Anyone got any ideas?'

For some reason, everyone looked at Archie, who was about to say that, no, he didn't have any ideas when . . .

'I don't believe it!' said a voice. 'What are you doing here, Archie?'

Looking round, Archie saw a man in green overalls driving a set of steps of the sort used to let people climb in and out of aeroplanes. It was, Archie realized, the burly man from the library protest on Wednesday, and he did not hesitate.

'Can you get Cyd and her mum to the main terminal?' he asked. 'In less than four minutes?'

'Course I can!' said the burly man cheerily. 'I can do anything for the lad who saved our library. Sit yourselves down on the steps and hang on tight!'

The burly man drove them at full speed across a runway towards the terminal building, narrowly missing a jumbo jet, almost overturning as he swung round the corner of the terminal building and then, two minutes later, screeching to a halt in front of the main entrance.

'Thank you,' said Archie, as he climbed

down from the ladder. 'We're very grateful for—'

'You haven't got time for all that,' said the burly man. 'You go and make sure your friends check in! Desk number twenty-two. Straight through those doors and over to the left!'

With the tall man carrying the luggage, Archie, Cyd and her mother raced through the glass doors, ran across the lobby and arrived, panting for breath, at desk number twenty-two.

'Are we too late?' asked Cyd's mother, 'for the flight to Miami?'

'Still a minute to go,' said the girl behind the desk with a smile. 'Do you have your tickets and your passports?'

'Yes,' said Cyd's mother, taking out her bag. 'Yes we do!'

'You did it, Archie!' said Cyd, and her eyes were shining as she looked at him. 'I don't know how, but you did it! And I will never

forget this. You are the best friend, absolutely the *best* friend, that anybody could ever have!'

And then, right there in the airport terminal, in front of everybody, she not only put her arms round Archie and hugged him, she gave him a big, smacking kiss on one side of his face, and then a big, smacking kiss on the other.

'I could be wrong,' said the tall man quietly, as they watched Cyd and her mother disappear through the gates to the departure lounge, 'but I think she likes you.'

The helicopter flew Archie home, and the old man with the bald head was waiting at the field to drive him back to his house in Garfield Crescent.

The day had, he thought, turned out

rather better than he'd expected. At least it
had until he got back to the house and his
mother met him in the hallway, carrying a pile
of magazines.

'One thing!' she said, sounding very fed
up. 'I ask you to do one *tiny* thing for me and,
three hours later, have you done it? No!'

She stormed out of the door.

'Honestly! I don't believe it, Archie!'